j PIC BK Houppert A.
Houppert, Anne Marie,
What about X? :an alphabet adventure /
9781419740787

5/2021

W9-AUY-664

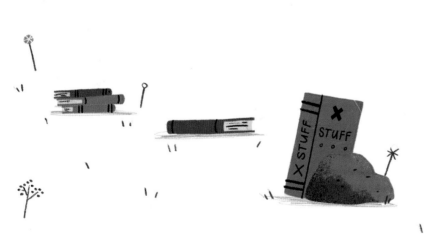

What About X?

An Alphabet Adventure

by Anne Marie Houppert

illustrated by Daniel Wiseman

ABRAMS APPLESEED
NEW YORK

It was a perfect day for a camping trip.

All the letters at the Alphabet Academy were excited, especially X.

X had never been camping!

"What should we bring?"
asked **Question Mark**.

X looked around at his friends.

A picked **a**pples for the bus ride.

B brought **b**inoculars for bird-watching.

C made a clatter with **c**anteens.

D helped load the **d**uffel bags.

E packed **e**ar plugs,
because *someone* snores.

F found the **f**ishing poles.

X pressed his nose against the window.
The bus was filling up with supplies.

G grabbed **g**raham crackers
for making s'mores.

"A **h**at for every head," **H** said.

Just then, **X** thought of
something he could bring.

An **X**-ray!

But what fun would an **X**-ray be on a camping trip?

"I'll bring **i**ce cream!" **I** screamed as she emptied ice trays into the cooler.

J juggled **j**uice boxes.

K flew a **k**ite as he ran toward the bus.

LMNO&**P** made a map with **l**ime green,
magenta, **n**avy blue, **o**range, and **p**urple markers.

A **quiver** full of arrows for archery, **Q** decided.

R wrestled with the **r**aft.

"**S**unscreen for sun safety," **S** said.

T trotted up with the **t**ent.

U packed **u**mbrellas
(just in case).

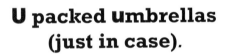

V tossed a **v**olleyball,
and **W** blew a **w**histle.

X was nowhere to be seen.

Y added a **y**ardstick to measure the *big* fish they would catch.

T AGADEMY

Z **z**ipped up the sleeping bags.

"What about **X**?" Question Mark asked.

X was running toward the treehouse.

He'd thought of the perfect thing to bring!

The xylophone!

They could play it
when they sang songs
around the campfire.

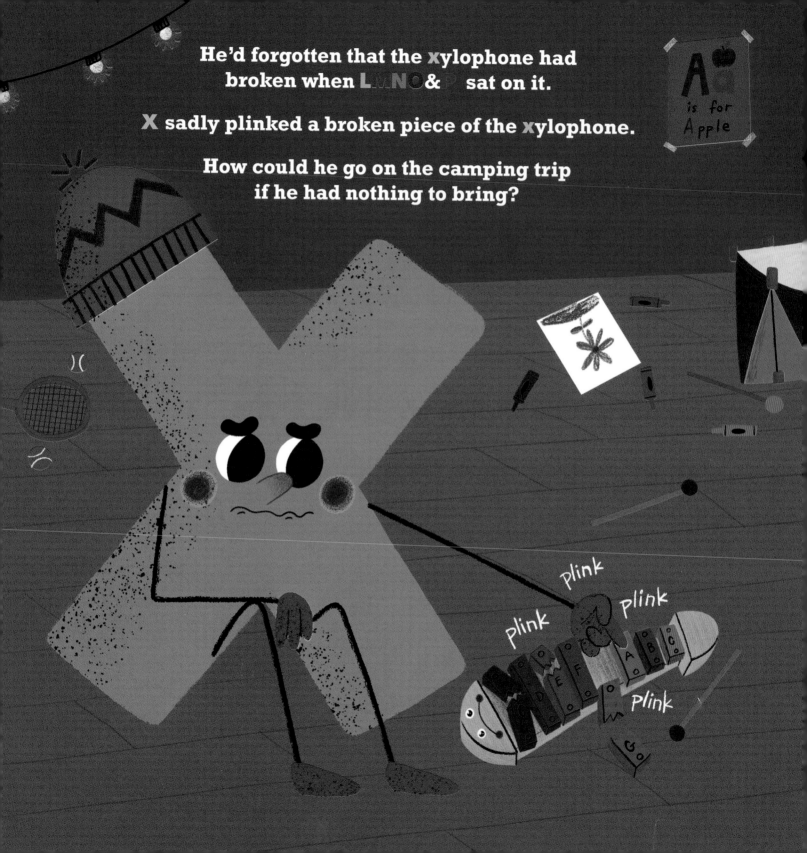

He'd forgotten that the xylophone had
broken when L M N O & P sat on it.

X sadly plinked a broken piece of the xylophone.

How could he go on the camping trip
if he had nothing to bring?

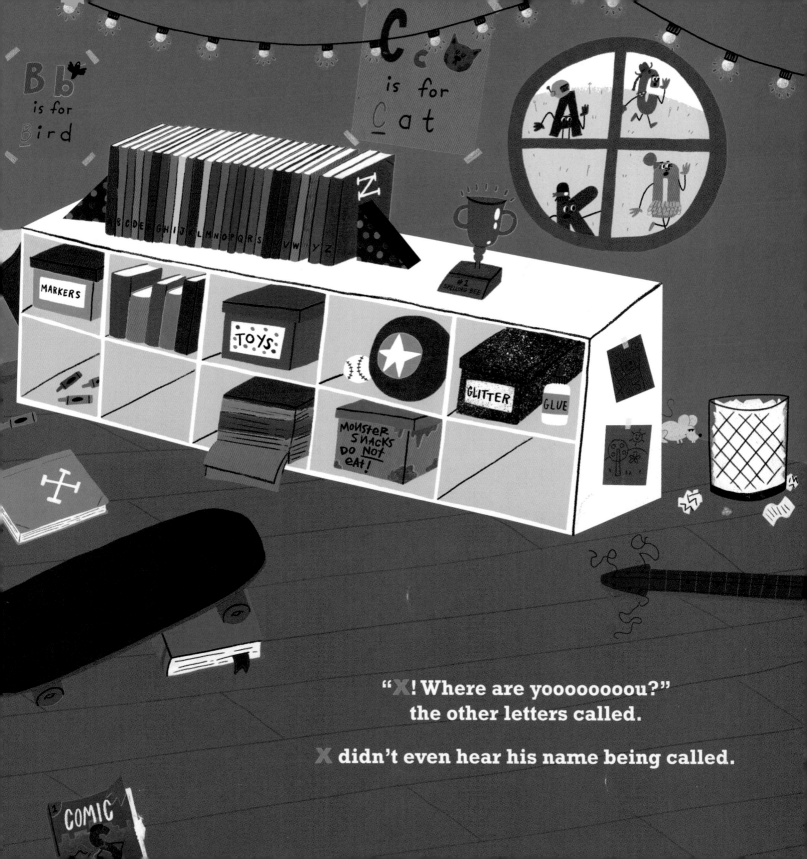

"X! Where are yooooooooou?"
the other letters called.

X didn't even hear his name being called.

"**X**! Where aaaaaaaaaare you?"
the letters shouted again.

X didn't know what to say.
He'd never thought of just bringing himself!

He would help them find exactly the right camping spot!

"Let's go!" yelled **X**.

Everyone cheered and raced to the bus.

Everyone except X.

He *cartwheeled* to the bus!

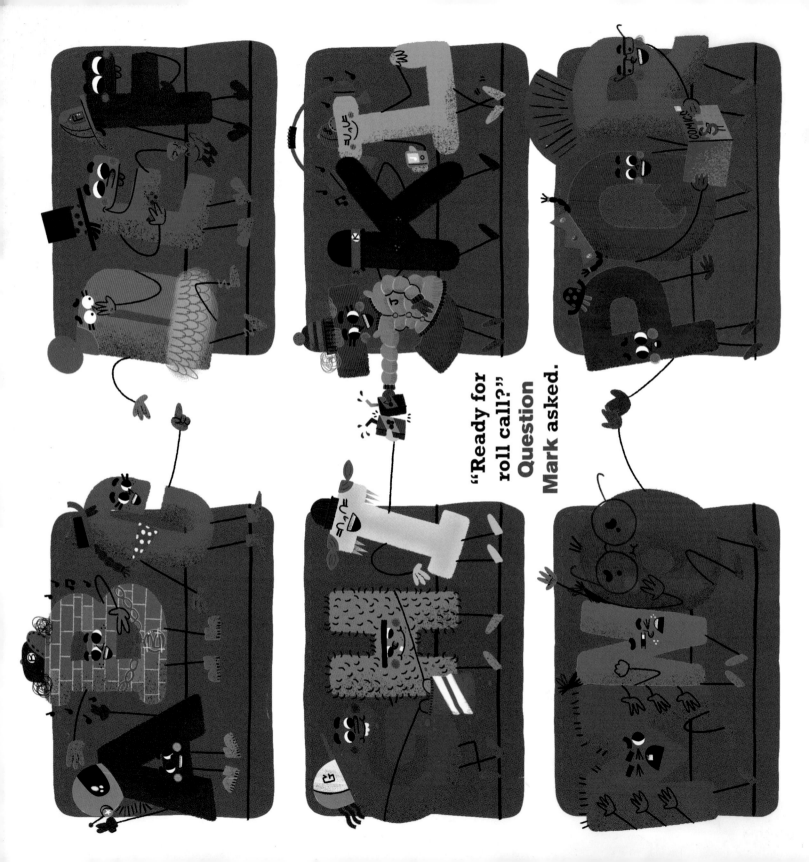

"Ready for roll call?" Question Mark asked.

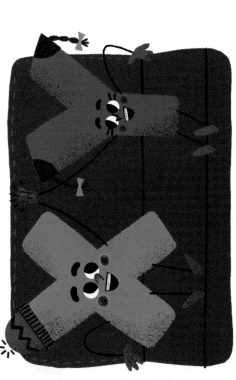

When it was his turn, X sang his name extra loud as he high-fived Y.

He could already tell it was going to be an exceptionally excellent trip.

ALPHABET ACADEMY

DOWNTOWN

PARAGRAPH PARK

PIZZA SHACK

ALICE AMPERSAND MEMORIAL

BEEP! BEEP!

STOP

AMY

DICTIONARY DOCKS

PHONICS FOREST

To my family, especially my mom,
who took us to the library a lot!
—A.M.H.

For my favorite camping buddy, Elizabeth
—D.W.